THE POISON PLOT

SWORD GIRL

THE POISON PLOT

FRANCES WATTS

ILLUSTRATED BY GREGORY ROGERS

ALLEN&UNWIN

First published in 2012

Allen & Unwin
83 Alexander Street
Crows Nest NSW 2065
Australia
Phone: (61 2) 8425 0100
Fax: (61 2) 9906 2218
Email: info@allenandunwin.com
Web: www.allenandunwin.com

A Cataloguing-in-Publication entry is available from the National Library of Australia
www.trove.nla.gov.au

ISBN 978 1 74237 792 6

Cover design by Seymour Designs
Cover illustration by Gregory Rogers
Text design by Seymour Designs
Set in 16/21 pt Adobe Jenson Pro by Seymour Designs
This book was printed in February 2012 at McPherson's Printing Group, 76 Nelson St, Maryborough, Victoria 3465, Australia.
www.mcphersonsprinting.com.au

10 9 8 7 6 5 4 3 2 1

For David, who had the sneezles

F. W.

For Matt

G. R.

CHAPTER 1

'Make way, make way! Fifty kinds of fresh fish coming through for the kitchen!'

It was early morning, and Tommy was crossing the great courtyard of Flamant Castle. She dodged out of the way of the cart clattering across the flagstones, only to hear someone behind her yell: 'Watch where you're going, girlie. I've got five hundred eggs in this basket!'

'Sorry,' Tommy said, as the egg woman barged past her.

The courtyard was busier than she'd ever seen it. She stepped out of the path of a man rolling two enormous rounds of cheese, as big as cart wheels.

'Poultry coming through: starlings, storks and swans!'

Tommy craned her head to look at the brace of birds the poultry man had slung around his neck. What was going on?

She had almost reached the armoury where she worked when she saw a small round man in brown robes. Despite all the activity in the courtyard, he was looking at the sky.

'Good morning, sir,' Tommy said to the physician.

'Eh?' said the physician. 'Oh, hello, Sword Girl. Have you seen the carrier pigeon?'

'No,' said Tommy. 'Not this morning.'

'Bother. I need some of his droppings for one of my cures.' The physician looked up at the sky again.

'Sir, why is the castle so busy this morning?' Tommy asked.

'Busy?' The physician looked around at the tradespeople hurrying to and fro. 'I suppose it must be something to do with the great banquet,' he said.

'A great banquet?' said Tommy, excited. 'What banquet?'

But the physician had wandered off. 'Where is that pigeon?' he was muttering to himself.

Maybe the blacksmith would know something about the great banquet, Tommy hoped.

She entered the armoury to see the blacksmith standing by the fire, softening a piece of armour that needed reshaping. Several shields and helmets were stacked

on the workbench, also in need of repair.

'Smith, have you heard about the great banquet?' Tommy asked.

The blacksmith looked up at her from under his bushy eyebrows. 'Oh aye, I've heard about it,' he said. 'But we've no time for feastin' here, Sword Girl. Sir Benedict and his men will be leaving tomorrow to patrol Sir Walter's lands. They'll need two dozen swords, so you'd better hop to it.'

'Yes, Smith,' said Tommy. 'Right away.' As Keeper of the Blades, it was her job to clean and sharpen all the bladed weapons of the castle.

She went through the door to the left of the fireplace into the sword chamber and quickly got to work. Pulling swords from the long rack against the wall opposite the door, she used a file and whetstone to sharpen the blades before polishing them with clove-scented oil.

'You're working hard this morning, dearie,' came a voice from a small rack of swords in the dimmest part of the room. It was one of the Old Wrecks. These were the swords that had never been carried into battle, and so were never used by the knights of Flamant Castle. They had been dusty and neglected when Tommy first started work in the sword chamber, but now their blades shone in the light of the candle flickering on the wall. What none of the knights knew – except Sir Benedict – was that the Old

Wrecks were inhabited by the spirits of their last owners.

Tommy glanced at the sabre which had spoken. 'Hello, Nursie,' she said. 'Smith told me that Sir Benedict is taking some of the knights out on a patrol tomorrow, so I have to get their swords ready.'

Sir Benedict was Flamant Castle's bravest knight, and he was responsible for the safety of the castle and lands belonging to Sir Walter the Bald and his wife, Lady Beatrix the Bored.

'A patrol, eh?' a deep voice boomed from a long-handled dagger. 'It sounds like trouble on the borders, if you ask me.'

'Well I didn't ask you, Bevan Brumm,' Nursie replied. 'What would you know about patrols? You were a merchant, not a knight.'

'I think Bevan Brumm might be right, though,' said another, younger voice. This was Jasper Swann. Jasper had been a squire, training to be a knight, before he fell ill and died. 'I heard some of the knights talking in here the other day and one of them said that Sir Malcolm the Mean had been trying to steal some of Sir Walter's land.'

'Who is Sir Malcolm the Mean?' Tommy wanted to know.

'He has the lands to the west of here,

dearie,' Nursie explained. 'But his own lands have never been enough for him. Oh no. He wants his neighbours' lands too.'

'He wants Sir Walter's lands?' exclaimed Tommy.

'Not just his lands, Sword Girl,' rumbled Bevan Brumm. 'Sir Malcolm the Mean wants Flamant Castle – and if Sir Benedict can't stop him at the border ...'

Tommy's heart started to pound. 'What?' she said. 'What will happen if Sir Benedict can't stop him?'

Bevan Brumm sounded grim. 'Flamant Castle will be at war.'

CHAPTER 2

FLAMANT CASTLE AT WAR! Tommy knew that noblemen often fought each other, but Flamant Castle had been at peace for many years.

Now that she understood how important Sir Benedict's patrol was, Tommy put extra care into preparing the swords. When she had finished sharpening and polishing each sword, she examined their blades again until she was sure they were as sharp as they could be.

By the time she had finished and stepped out into the courtyard she was tired and hungry, but before she headed over to the kitchen for dinner she decided to find Lil. The cat knew everything that went on in the castle – she would surely know if the castle was close to war.

Tommy scanned the courtyard, but Lil, who usually spent the afternoons napping on a sun-warmed flagstone, was nowhere to be seen. Perhaps all the day's activity had disturbed her and she had found somewhere quieter to sleep. Before she went through the low arch leading out of the courtyard, Tommy looked up at the battlements. Normally she didn't think twice before leaving the castle walls, but now she was glad to see the guards keeping watch. Suddenly the world outside the castle didn't seem as safe.

Tommy slipped through the castle gate and ran to the edge of the moat which encircled the castle walls. She looked left and right, and spotted the black and white cat sitting a little way off. As Tommy approached she could see that Lil was talking to the crocodiddle who lived in the moat. The crocodiddle, who usually wore a giant grin, seemed very quiet today.

'Lil, I've been looking for you everywhere,' said Tommy when she drew near. She turned to the crocodiddle. 'How are you, Mr Crocodiddle?'

The crocodiddle fixed a mournful gaze

on Tommy. 'Hello, Sword Girl. I was just telling Lil that I—*aaaahhh-CHOO!*' His giant wet sneeze almost drenched the cat.

'Do you mind?' said Lil, shaking herself.

'I can't help it,' said the crocodiddle miserably. 'I've got the sneezles.'

'You poor thing,' said Tommy sympathetically.

'I know,' moaned the crocodiddle. Then he sank so low into the moat that only his beady yellow eyes were visible. Every now and then a burst of bubbles told Tommy that he was sneezing underwater.

'So why were you looking for me?' Lil asked.

Tommy told Lil about Sir Benedict's patrol and her conversation with the Old Wrecks. 'Is it true that Sir Malcolm the

Mean wants to take over Flamant Castle?'

Lil nodded slowly. 'It is true,' she said. 'And it's true that some of his knights have been seen on Sir Walter's land. But you shouldn't be too worried about it, Tommy. There's not another knight around here that could beat Sir Benedict in a fight and everyone knows that. Not even Sir Malcolm would be foolish enough to send his knights into battle against Flamant Castle.'

Relieved, Tommy made her way back through the castle gate, Lil at her side.

'I hope it's a little more peaceful in the courtyard now,' said Lil, 'after all that commotion this morning. I suppose I won't get much sleep till after the great banquet.'

The banquet! Tommy had been so worried about Sir Malcolm the Mean she had forgotten all about it.

'Tell me about the banquet, Lil,' she said. 'Who's it for?'

'It's for Sir Percy the Pink,' the cat said. 'From Roses Castle, to the east of here. I suspect Sir Walter has decided that with Sir Malcolm making trouble, he should build up alliances with other noblemen. In three days' time Sir Percy and two hundred of his knights will be coming here for a great feast.'

When they reached the courtyard, it was almost deserted. Lil found a ray of sunshine from the setting sun in a quiet corner, and with a happy sigh sank onto a flagstone and began her bath.

Tommy bade her goodnight then ran across the courtyard to the kitchen to get her dinner.

The courtyard may have been quiet, but the kitchen was in an uproar.

The table where Tommy normally had her dinner was being used by a dozen kitchen girls with rolling pins, rolling out pastry. Mrs Moon, the cook, was standing by the massive fireplace. She was turning a wild boar on a spit, pausing occasionally to stir something bubbling in a giant cauldron. Tommy breathed in the rich aroma of meat and herbs.

'That smells delicious, Mrs Moon,' she said.

'Don't you be getting underfoot now, Thomasina,' Mrs Moon said sternly. 'We have four hundred venison pies to make this evening. You'll have to eat your soup over there.' She nodded towards a bowl of soup resting on a stool tucked into a corner of the kitchen.

The soup was almost cold, but Tommy didn't mind. She perched on the stool and

17

looked around curiously. As well as the usual meat, fish and eggs, there were some strange-looking foods.

'What are those?' Tommy asked, pointing to a bench.

Mrs Moon mopped some sweat from her brow and looked over. 'Those are figs and dates from over the sea. I'm going to put them in a bread pudding.'

'And what about those?' Tommy pointed to some orange and yellow balls. 'They look too tough to eat.'

'Those are oranges and lemons, from the south lands. You have to peel them before you eat them.'

'What are – eek!' Tommy lifted her feet into the air as a sack at the base of her stool began to move. 'What's in there?'

'Eels.'

'Yuck.' Tommy shivered and hugged her

knees to her chest. She opened her mouth to ask another question but Mrs Moon had run out of patience.

'If you don't stop peppering me with questions, Thomasina,' the cook said, 'I'll tell Sir Benedict that I need you in the kitchen to help prepare for the banquet. You'll be polishing knives instead of swords before you know it.'

With a gulp, Tommy clamped her lips shut. She loved being Keeper of the Blades more than anything. Surely Mrs Moon wouldn't really make her come back to the kitchen? She decided not to wait around to find out.

'Goodnight, Mrs Moon,' she said, then slipped off to bed.

CHAPTER 3

THE NEXT MORNING the courtyard was busy again, and Tommy watched with interest as a cart stacked with barrels manoeuvred through the low arch leading from the castle gate.

'What's in your barrels?' she asked the driver as she stopped to pat his horse's neck.

'I've got wine, ale and cider for the banquet,' he replied. 'Nothing for little girls.'

'I'm not a little girl!' Tommy said. 'I'm Keeper of the Blades.'

'Begging your pardon,' said the driver. 'That's an important job. Surprised they've got a little girl to do it.' He chuckled as Tommy sniffed and stalked off.

When she got to the armoury, Smith's pile of armour waiting for repair seemed to have grown. 'How do they expect me to equip them for patrol if they keep bashing around the armour during practice?' he grumbled. 'How are you going with those swords, girl?'

'They're all ready, Smith.'

'Good. Bring 'em out here then.' He pointed his hammer at an empty sword rack against the wall.

Tommy carefully carried the swords

she'd prepared out into the armoury, giving each blade a last polish before she slipped it into the rack.

She'd just returned to the sword chamber when a voice behind her said, 'Excuse me, Sword Girl.' It was the physician. 'I was wondering if you would sharpen my sickle for me? I need to cut some herbs for a cure I'm making for Lady Beatrix, but my sickle is blunt.'

'Yes, of course,' said Tommy. As she began to file the blade she remembered someone else who needed a cure. 'Sir, do you know a cure for colds?' she asked.

'A cure for colds, let me see …' The physician put his chin in his hand and stared at the ceiling. 'If I was suffering from a cold I'd mix freshly squeezed orange juice with pigeon droppings, and paint it on my nose. Of course, oranges are hard to come by.'

Not at the moment they weren't! Tommy could make a cure for the crocodiddle. As soon as the physician had left the sword chamber, she found an empty pot that had once held oil for polishing the swords and ran out into the courtyard.

'Where are you off to in such a hurry?' asked Lil, who was basking in the sunshine against the wall of the armoury.

'I'm looking for the pigeon,' said Tommy. 'The physician just told me a cure for colds – I want to make it for the crocodiddle.'

'I'm sure he'll appreciate it,' said Lil, closing her eyes. 'I thought I saw the pigeon hanging around the turret up there.' She

stretched a paw towards a small, high tower built on top of a larger tower.

'Thanks,' said Tommy, and she took off up the winding stone stairs.

When she stepped out at the top of the tower the courtyard below was so small she could barely see Lil by the armoury wall. She walked over to the battlements and peered through a gap. She saw the town on the other side of the moat, then the farmers' fields, and beyond that the countryside stretching away into the distance. Sir Walter owned the land as far as she could see, Tommy knew.

Looking up to the top of the turret, she called, 'Pigeon? Are you there?'

There was a pause, then a cautious voice said, 'Who wants to know?'

'It's me, Tommy – the sword girl.'

The pigeon swooped down and perched on the battlements beside Tommy. 'What do you want?'

'Um …' Tommy hesitated. She knew the carrier pigeon found it insulting to be asked for his droppings. 'Well I want to make a cure, and I need …'

The pigeon groaned. 'You need my droppings,' he finished.

'I'm sorry,' Tommy said. 'It's for the crocodiddle. He's got a terrible cold.'

'You're telling me.' The pigeon rolled his eyes. 'I was flying low above the moat when he sneezed. I thought I'd been caught in a thunderstorm! My feathers got all wet.'

'He looked so miserable when I saw him yesterday,' Tommy said.

'All right,' the pigeon said with a
'I'll help you. But—' he pointed a wing at
Tommy, 'you're not allowed to watch.'

Tommy held out her pot with one hand
and covered her eyes with the other.

A few seconds later the pigeon said,
'There you go. And it had better work the

first time because I'm not giving you any more of my droppings.'

'Thank you,' Tommy said as the pigeon swooped off the battlements and soared into the sky. Now she had the droppings, all she needed was an orange. Surely Mrs Moon wouldn't miss one orange …

There were dozens of people bustling around the kitchen when Tommy entered. Mrs Moon was busy directing them. Tommy started to explain about the crocodiddle and his cold, but the cook interrupted her. 'I don't have time to listen to your stories now, Thomasina. Just take whatever you need and go.'

Back in the sword chamber, Tommy asked Bevan Brumm for his help, and used the long-handled dagger to halve

the orange. Then she squeezed the juice into the pot with the droppings. She was stirring the mixture with a wooden paddle when she was surprised by an unpleasant voice at the door.

'What's that disgusting smell?'

Spinning around, Tommy saw horrible Reynard, Keeper of the Bows.

'Ah, the disgusting smell must be you, Sword Girl.' He laughed unkindly then disappeared.

'A thoroughly nasty boy,' said Nursie.

'You are not wrong,' said Bevan Brumm.

'I know I'm not wrong,' said Nursie. 'That's why I said it. Really, Bevan Brumm, you say the most ridiculous things sometimes.'

'I'm just glad Sir Benedict didn't make him Keeper of the Blades,' Jasper Swann said. Reynard had never forgiven Tommy for getting the job he wanted. 'But he's right about the smell. What is that you're mixing up there, Sword Girl?'

'A cure for the crocodiddle's cold,' said Tommy. 'And I think it's ready.'

Taking the pot, she walked through the castle gate and across the grass to the moat.

There was no sign of the crocodiddle.

'Crocodiddle?' she called. 'Mr Crocodiddle, are you there?'

The surface of the water shivered as the crocodiddle raised his head. His beady yellow eyes were dull. 'Hello,' he said pitifully. '*Aaah-chooo!*'

Tommy sprang back just in time to avoid a soaking.

'Mr Crocodiddle, I've made a cure for your sneezles. I got the recipe from the physician.' She held out the pot.

'A cure for me?' The crocodiddle looked hopeful. 'That's very – *aaaah-CHOO!* – kind of you, Sword Girl.'

'I have to paint it on your nose,' Tommy explained.

The crocodiddle placed his nose on the bank of the moat and Tommy spread the smelly orange mixture on it with her wooden paddle. She had just finished when she heard a bellow coming from the castle.

'SWORD GIRL! Where are you?'

'That sounds like Smith,' Tommy said. 'I'd better go.' Taking the pot she ran towards the castle gate. 'I hope the cure works,' she called over her shoulder.

CHAPTER 4

'SWORD GIRL!'

'Coming, Smith!' Tommy bolted into the armoury, out of breath after sprinting all the way from the moat.

'There you are,' said Smith. He wrinkled his nose and shot a curious look at the pot in Tommy's hand, but he didn't ask any questions. 'Sword Girl, I need you to go to town. I sent Reynard to the forge with an order for more helmets, but I forgot to add shields. You're to go tell the blacksmith I need a dozen bucklers. Got that?'

'Yes, Smith – a dozen bucklers,' Tommy repeated.

'And if you see Reynard, tell him to hurry back and no loafing about with the town lads.'

Tommy nodded, though she knew that if she did see Reynard in town she'd do her best to keep out of his way. She went to the sword chamber to put down her pot.

'Smith is sending me to town!' she told the Old Wrecks. As a kitchen girl, she hardly ever went to town. This would be her first time going on her own.

'That's a very responsible job,' Nursie said.

'Mind you do your duty well,' Bevan Brumm advised her.

'Then hurry back and tell us everything you've seen,' said Jasper, who sounded as excited as Tommy felt.

Tommy's excitement mounted as she walked across the bridge over the moat. Halfway across she stopped and looked back at the castle. With its sturdy walls and soaring towers, it looked mighty and impenetrable. The flags atop the towers fluttered in the breeze, showing the flamingo that was Sir Walter's crest. Tommy smiled as she stepped off the bridge and followed the road through the fields to the town gates.

She had thought the courtyard was busy, but it looked sleepy compared to the town. Tommy walked down a narrow street lined with wooden houses all jammed together. Some of the houses had stables out the front, and she could see oxen in their stalls. There were also shops among the houses, with signs to show what they sold.

It took her a while to find the forge, as she had to keep stopping to ask people the way, but at last she found it on the other side of a market square almost as big as the castle's great courtyard. She gave the blacksmith Smith's order then walked back towards the town gate. She was dawdling a bit, watching a merchant who had spilled a sack of grain hopping up and down in fury as three pigs snuffled up his wares, when she caught sight of a stocky boy with red hair.

Tommy turned away quickly but it was too late; Reynard had seen her.

'Look,' he yelled to his two friends. 'It's that kitchen girl who took my job.'

The smaller boy picked up a rock and threw it at Tommy.

'Ouch!' Tommy cried as the rock grazed her arm.

'Smelly Sword Girl!' Reynard jeered.

When Reynard's other friend stooped to pick up a stick, she took off at a run.

'After her!' she heard Reynard call.

CHAPTER 5

TOMMY RACED DOWN the street, weaving between the carts and people blocking her path. She could still hear the jeers of Reynard and his friends behind her.

She stopped at a corner, unsure which way to go. To her left was a tavern with a golden prawn hanging above the doorway. The words THE PICKLED PRAWN were written on the sign in fancy letters.

Tommy ducked down a narrow alley beside the tavern and crouched behind a barrel. She sat there for a few minutes, panting.

When she thought it was probably safe, she started to rise, but an oily voice coming through the open window above her head made her freeze.

'And when we have poisoned Sir Walter,' hissed the voice, 'we'll invade his lands.'

'I see,' said a second voice uncertainly. 'Could you just explain it to me – *aaaah-choo!* – again?'

Poison Sir Walter? Tommy drew in her breath. Surely she must have misheard.

'On the night of the banquet,' said the oily voice, 'you make sure you get close to Sir Walter, and slip this pill into his mug of cider.'

'Are you sure – *ah-choo!* Oh bother, where's my handkerchief ... Are you sure he drinks cider?'

'Or his tankard of ale,' said the oily voice.

The second man blew his nose loudly then said, 'What if he doesn't drink ale?'

'Into his goblet of wine then!' The oily voice was sounding impatient now.

'Okay, so I put the poison pill into his cider, or his ale, or his wine ... and then what?'

'Then you come out to the hiding place I showed you last night, by the moat, and tell me that you've done it. And I'll ride back to

Malice Castle and tell Sir Malcolm. When Sir Walter drops dead after the banquet, the knights of Flamant Castle will think Sir Percy the Pink and his knights are to blame. And while Sir Benedict's men are off fighting the knights of Roses Castle, Sir Malcolm will invade.' The oily voice snickered. 'And Flamant Castle will be ours!'

'And what – *aaah-choo!* – do I get again?'

'For goodness' sake, stop that sneezing and sniffling. It's very distracting.'

'I can't stop!' cried the second plotter in frustration. 'I wish I could. But I've caught a terrible cold.' He gave a loud sniffle. 'It's all your fault for making me sneak around outside Flamant Castle in the middle of the night when I should have been tucked up in bed.'

Sneaking around outside the castle? He must have caught the cold from the crocodiddle, Tommy realised.

'You'll get lots of gold and treasure,' the oily voice said soothingly.

'That'll be a nice change,' sniffed the plotter with the cold. 'All I ever get from Sir Percy is a boff on the head. And he calls me Sir Blockhead.'

'Sir Malcolm will be very grateful for your assistance,' the oily plotter promised.

'*AAAH-CHOO!*'

This last, loudest sneeze seemed to mark the end of the conversation. Tommy, who had been frozen to the spot under the window, stood up. She peered cautiously over the window frame, but the table by the window was empty. The plotters had gone.

Tommy began to run. She had to get back to the castle to tell Sir Benedict about the plot. She just hoped he hadn't yet left on his patrol.

Down the narrow streets and through the town gate she raced. Crossing the bridge over the moat she had forgotten all about the crocodiddle until a giant sneeze made her jump.

'Oh, poor Mr Crocodiddle,' she said, leaning over the side of the bridge. The crocodiddle's nose was still painted orange with the cure Tommy had made. 'How are your sneezles?'

'No better,' moaned the crocodiddle. He gave a loud sniffle.

'I'm sorry,' Tommy said. 'I really hoped the cure would work.' Shaking her head in disappointment, she ran through the castle gate and across the courtyard to the armoury.

Smith was hammering the dent out of a shield, the *clang, clang, clang* ringing off the stone walls.

'Smith,' Tommy panted. 'Have you seen Sir Benedict?'

The blacksmith stilled his hammer. 'What's that, Sword Girl?'

'Sir Benedict,' Tommy repeated. 'Have you seen him?'

'Aye, I've seen him.'

Tommy breathed a sigh of relief.

But Smith continued, 'He was here with the knights to pick up their swords and armour just after you went off to town. They rode off on their patrol a good hour ago.'

'Oh no!' Tommy said.

Smith gave Tommy a puzzled look. 'There's no need to be upset, Sword Girl. Sir Benedict was very impressed with the swords. You should be pleased.' He shook his hammer at Tommy.

Tommy tried to smile. 'That's – that's great,' she said. 'It's just that ...' She was about to tell Smith about the plot, then hesitated. Smith never left the armoury. What could he do to foil Sir Malcolm's plot? No, with Sir Benedict gone, she could think of only one other person who could help. And she wasn't even a person ...

Tommy dashed out into the courtyard. 'Lil? Lil, where are you?'

'Over here, Tommy.'

The cat was lying on a low wall beside a stairwell that led down to the cellars. She sprang to her feet, alert, as Tommy approached.

'What is it?' she asked.

'A plot!' said Tommy. 'Sir Malcolm the Mean is plotting to poison Sir Walter and make it look like the work of Sir Percy the Pink. Then Sir Malcolm is going to take over Flamant Castle while our knights are off fighting with Sir Percy!'

'Tell me everything,' urged Lil.

Tommy sat on the wall beside the cat and repeated the conversation she'd heard while hiding beneath the tavern window.

When she was finished, Lil said, 'Did you see what the plotters looked like? Did you hear their names?'

Tommy shook her head. 'All I know is that the one who'll be at the banquet is one of Sir Percy's knights. He has a cold, and Sir Percy calls him "Sir Blockhead".'

'Hmm. That doesn't give us much to go on,' said Lil. 'And Sir Benedict won't be back from his patrol till the evening of the banquet, the day after tomorrow.'

'We have to stop the banquet!' Tommy declared.

But Lil shook her head. 'That's impossible,' she said. 'And anyway, I think we'd better keep this to ourselves, Tommy. We don't want to scare the plotters off; they'd only try again. No, we want to catch them red-handed.' She groomed her whiskers thoughtfully. At last she said, 'You'll have to go back to town tomorrow morning and try to find Sir Blockhead with the poison pill. Then you can describe him to Sir Benedict before he goes in to the banquet.'

Tommy felt a stab of fear at the thought of coming face to face with the plotters, but she knew Lil was right. If they wanted to foil the plot, it was up to her.

CHAPTER 6

As soon as she arrived at the armoury the next morning, Tommy said to Smith, 'I thought I might run into town to check when those new shields will be ready.'

'Good idea, Sword Girl,' Smith said.

Phew! Tommy set off at once. Crossing the courtyard, she worried about the task ahead. Even if she did find Sir Blockhead, how could she describe him to Sir Benedict so that the knight would recognise him? She could say he had brown hair – but there might be two hundred knights at the banquet with brown hair! And the plotter had a cold – there might be dozens of knights with colds! Maybe the plan she and Lil had come up with wasn't such a good one after all ...

As she passed through the castle gate, still lost in thought, she heard a voice calling her from the moat.

'Hey, Sword Girl!'

Tommy ran onto the bridge and looked down at the crocodiddle.

'How are you feeling today?' she asked.

The crocodiddle beamed. 'That cure for the sneezles worked!'

'You do look much better,' said Tommy.

'You can probably wash the cure off now.'

'What? I already did.'

'But … your nose,' said Tommy.

The crocodiddle frowned. 'What about my nose?'

'It's orange.'

'Orange? What are you talking about?' The crocodiddle swam over to a calm, glassy patch of water. He gazed at his reflection then let out a shriek. 'Eek! My nose is orange!'

He dipped his nose in the water and began to scrub at it furiously with a giant claw. He looked at his reflection again. 'Still orange!' he wailed. 'What am I going to do?'

'I'll ask the physician as soon as I get back from town,' Tommy promised.

Oh dear, Tommy thought, as she reached

the town gate. She hoped the physician knew a cure for the cure. She'd feel terrible if, in trying to cure her friend's cold, she had turned his nose permanently orange.

Suddenly she stopped as an idea struck her. Then she turned and ran all the way back to the armoury.

'I forgot something,' she called to Smith breathlessly as she dashed past him on her way to the sword chamber.

There she snatched up the pot with the orange cure and raced back to town. Through the crowded streets she ran until she saw the sign with the golden prawn. She hoped that this might be the plotters' regular meeting place.

Tommy loitered outside the door of the tavern for nearly an hour but no one

entered. She was about to give up when she heard a series of sneezes.

Two men were approaching.

'I feel worse today than I did yesterday,' said a small brown-haired man. He honked into a handkerchief then said, 'I might be too ill to attend the banquet.'

Beside him, a tall thin man with oily black hair said in an oily voice, 'There, there. A hearty beef pie in The Pickled Prawn will do wonders, you'll see.'

It was the plotters! As they reached the door, Tommy stepped forward. 'That's a terrible cold you have there, sir,' she said to the brown-haired man.

'It's the worst cold I ever had,' Sir Blockhead agreed.

'I don't mean to bother you, sir,' Tommy

said, 'only I happen to have a cure here that the castle's physician made for my poor sick grandmother. I'm sure Grandma could spare a drop for you, sir.'

'A cure? A cure, you say? *Aaah-CHOO!* Well give it here, girl, and be quick about it.'

'Just bend down, sir, and I'll apply the cure.'

When Sir Blockhead leaned forward, Tommy dipped the small wooden paddle into her pot and painted his nose.

'His nose is orange,' the oily plotter observed when she was done.

'Yes, sir, that's part of the cure,' Tommy said. 'You need to leave it on for a day and a night.'

'That's all right,' the oily plotter said to

his companion in a low voice. 'You can wash it off just before you go to the banquet tomorrow evening.'

'*Aaaah-CHOO!*' Sir Blockhead replied.

CHAPTER 7

ON THE DAY of the banquet Tommy woke with butterflies in her stomach that wouldn't go away.

She would have gone mad with the agony of waiting if she hadn't been kept so busy. First Sir Walter came to the sword chamber to tell her that he wanted to wear his favourite sword to the banquet. Sir Walter was very proud of his sword. It was studded with rubies, and the blade was beautifully engraved with flamingos.

Tommy set to work polishing the sword, and also cleaned swords for the many other knights who came to the sword chamber during the day to select swords to wear that evening.

Whenever she had a spare moment, she would run out to the courtyard to see if Sir Benedict and his knights had returned yet, only to be disappointed.

'Where could they be?' Tommy asked Lil in frustration as the sun started to sink below the battlements. Lil had once again positioned herself on the low wall, where she had a good view of the archway leading from the castle gate. 'The banquet will be starting soon.'

'Don't worry,' Lil said. 'They'll be here.' But it seemed to Tommy that the cat's green eyes were anxious.

The shadows in the courtyard were long when a thunder of hooves could be heard clattering over the bridge to the castle gate. And then the courtyard was filled with men and horses. Not only had Sir Benedict's patrol returned, Sir Percy and his knights from Roses Castle had arrived for the banquet at the same time.

'Sir Benedict!' Tommy called when she caught sight of the tall, dark-haired knight.

But Sir Walter grasped Sir Benedict's sleeve the moment the knight dismounted from his horse. 'I thought you weren't going to make it in time,' the nobleman said. 'Quick, get changed and come to the banqueting hall at once.'

'Yes, sir,' said Sir Benedict. He shot an apologetic look at Tommy, and hurried off.

Tommy turned to Lil in despair. 'What do we do now?' she asked. She kicked a flagstone in frustration. 'If only I was still a kitchen girl,' she muttered. 'Then I could have found a reason to enter the banqueting hall.' She thought about this for a minute. 'It's worth a try,' she declared.

Tommy ran through the kitchen door. 'Mrs Moon,' she said, 'I have to get into the banqueting hall to speak to Sir Benedict. It's urgent!'

The cook was ladling soup into large wooden bowls. 'You leave Sir Benedict alone, Thomasina. He's a very important man.'

'Please, Mrs Moon,' Tommy begged. 'It's a matter of life and death.'

Something in her voice must have convinced the cook, because she stopped what she was doing and looked Tommy in the eye.

'Are you sure about that, Thomasina?' she asked.

Tommy nodded. 'The fate of Flamant Castle depends on me getting a message to Sir Benedict.'

'Very well,' Mrs Moon decided. 'When the girls are serving the soup, you can take Sir Benedict's bowl.' She looked Tommy up and down. 'But you can't go into the banqueting hall dressed like that.'

Tommy never would have thought she'd be glad to exchange her tunic and

leggings for her old kitchen-girl dress, but tonight she was glad to put the dress on. She presented herself for Mrs Moon's inspection.

'Dear me, haven't you mended that tear in your dress yet?' The cook clucked her tongue then untied her own apron and slipped it over Tommy's head. It reached almost to Tommy's ankles, but at least it covered her torn dress. 'That'll have to do,' said Mrs Moon. 'Now go join the other girls.'

The banqueting hall was noisy and crowded when Tommy entered, carrying a bowl of soup. With four hundred knights crammed

around dozens of tables, it was hard to recognise anyone. She just hoped her plan had worked and that Sir Benedict would be able to find a knight with an orange nose. The physician had said that the orange would fade after a couple of days.

She scanned the room until she saw who she was looking for, then squeezed between the tables to where Sir Benedict sat.

'Your soup, sir.' Tommy put the steaming bowl down in front of the knight.

He looked at her in surprise. 'Tommy? What are you doing dressed as a serving girl?'

'Sir, there's a plot to poison Sir Walter,' Tommy whispered urgently. 'You have to stop it.'

If Sir Benedict was surprised, he didn't

show it. 'Meet me in the courtyard in five minutes,' he said calmly.

'Yes, sir.' Tommy raced back to the kitchen, pausing just long enough to return the cook's apron. 'Thank you, Mrs Moon,' she called over her shoulder. She stopped in her quarters to pull off her dress and slip back into her tunic and leggings, then she hurried out into the courtyard.

She sat with Lil on the low wall, and when Sir Benedict joined them a few minutes later Tommy and the cat quickly outlined both the plot and Tommy's plan.

'So I look for the fellow with the orange nose?' Sir Benedict confirmed. 'Excellent plan, Tommy. Now here's what we're going to do when I find him …'

CHAPTER 8

Tommy stood in the sword chamber, clutching Jasper Swann in one hand. She was so nervous that her hand was shaking, but Jasper said, 'Relax, Sword Girl. You'll be fine.'

His quiet voice gave her confidence. When Sir Benedict entered the sword chamber ten minutes later, Tommy was ready.

'So kind of you to agree to a private chat,' Sir Benedict was saying. 'You've met our Keeper of the Blades before, I think?' he asked Sir Blockhead.

The knight tilted his head to one side, as if he recognised Tommy but couldn't quite remember where he had seen her before. Then his hand flew to his nose. 'You're the girl with the cure,' he said. 'You fixed my cold, but I can't get rid of the orange stain.'

'That was the idea,' Tommy said. With a steady hand, she raised her sword so it was level with Sir Blockhead's belly.

'What are you doing?' the knight blustered. 'Really, Sir Benedict, I must protest—'

'Hold your tongue,' Sir Benedict ordered. He searched the knight's pockets. 'Aha!'

He withdrew a pill. 'Is this the pill you were going to use to poison Sir Walter?'

Sir Blockhead turned pale. 'It wasn't my idea!' he cried. 'It was Sir Silas, from Malice Castle.'

'And where is Sir Silas hiding?' Sir Benedict demanded.

'In the bushes by the western wall of the castle,' Sir Blockhead gulped.

'Tommy, watch him,' Sir Benedict ordered. 'If he tries anything, you know what to do.'

Tommy tightened her grip on her sword. 'Yes, Sir Benedict,' she said.

And then Tommy was left alone with the culprit.

The knight looked from Tommy to her sword and back again. 'You're just a girl,' he sneered. 'What would you know about handling a sword?' He strode towards the door.

Tommy's heart was racing, but she didn't falter. 'Get back!' she said, thrusting her blade at him.

Sir Blockhead retreated, muttering

angrily, only to spin around suddenly and rush at Tommy.

'Out of my way, girl,' he cried. 'I'm warning you!'

As he drew near, Tommy gripped the sword tight and swung it with all her might.

With a yelp, Sir Blockhead leaped back, only narrowly avoiding the slash of sharpened steel. 'You could have hurt me!' he protested.

He moved off to sulk in the corner while Tommy patrolled the doorway, wishing Sir Benedict would hurry up.

'Well done, Sword Girl,' she heard someone say in a low voice. It was Jasper.

'Thanks,' she whispered back.

When at last Sir Benedict returned, he was accompanied by a very grumpy-looking Sir Silas, and Sir Hugh, another of Flamant Castle's knights. Sir Hugh had the point of his sword pressed into Sir Silas's back.

Sir Silas and the knights of Flamant Castle were followed into the sword chamber by Sir Walter, Sir Percy and two of the knights from Roses Castle.

Sir Percy stepped forward and glared at the traitor. 'You're in big trouble, Blockhead,' he said, then boffed the cowering knight

on the head. 'Take him back to Roses Castle and throw him in the dungeon,' he instructed his men.

'And you can throw Sir Silas into our own dungeon, Sir Hugh,' Sir Walter added.

'It's a good thing Sir Benedict uncovered the plot,' Sir Percy said to Sir Walter as the knights and their captives left the room. 'Or we might have been at war by sunrise tomorrow. But now I intend to send a message to Sir Malcolm the Mean: if he tries to invade Flamant Castle, he'll have to fight the knights of Roses Castle too.'

When Sir Percy had left the sword chamber, Sir Benedict turned to Sir Walter. 'Actually, sir,' he said, 'it wasn't me who uncovered the plot. It was Tommy.' He put his hand on Tommy's shoulder.

'Is that right?' said Sir Walter. 'Well, well, Sword Girl, you certainly deserve a reward for your excellent efforts. What shall it be?'

Tommy hesitated. Should she reveal her secret dream? She took a deep breath and said, 'When I'm old enough, sir, I would like to become a squire and train to be a knight.'

Sir Walter raised his eyebrows. 'A girl squire, eh? Hmm. It's not the normal way of things. But you keep up the good work, Sword Girl, and we'll see what we can do. Now, Sir Benedict, let's return to the banquet before all the venison pies are gone.'

Sir Benedict winked at Tommy, and followed Sir Walter from the room.

Although she was exhausted and longing for bed, Tommy remained behind to polish Jasper Swann.

Tommy had just replaced Jasper in the rack alongside the other Old Wrecks when she heard a cough. She turned to see a serving girl almost staggering under the weight of an enormous tray.

'Excuse me, miss,' said the girl. 'I've come from the banquet hall. Sir Benedict told me to bring this tray to the sword girl, with his compliments.'

'For ... for me?' Tommy sat on the floor and the serving girl placed the tray in front of her. 'Thank you,' she called as the girl slipped from the room.

Tommy gazed at the tray in wonder. She saw a whole venison pie on one plate, and

a huge wedge of cheese on another. There was a big slice of bread pudding, studded with raisins and dates. There was an apple tart smelling of cinnamon, and a steaming mug of hot apple cider. A  bowl of plums stewed in rosewater sat next to a dish of strawberries and cream. There was another dish filled only with cream alongside a plate of sardines. These, Tommy guessed, were for Lil.

As Lil picked daintily at the fish, Tommy pushed her fork through the crust of the venison pie to release a delicious aroma of nutmeg and cloves. 'Yum!' she exclaimed. 'Wasn't it nice of Sir Benedict to think of us?'

Lil lifted her head from her dish. 'It's because you're a hero, Tommy.'

Nursie spoke up. 'Did you hear what Sir Walter said? He might let our sword girl become a squire! I told you she'd be the first-ever girl squire.' She cackled with glee. 'Didn't I tell you, Bevan Brumm?'

'You were not wrong,' said Bevan Brumm in a dignified voice. 'And it is an honour richly deserved.'

'An honour richly deserved?' said Nursie. 'What does that mean when it's at home?'

Jasper Swann spoke up. 'I think Bevan Brumm means that Tommy is the best sword girl ever.'

And on that they all agreed.

Do you know
how Tommy became
Keeper of the Blades?
Read about her first
adventure in

THE SECRET
OF THE
Swords

CHAPTER I

'THOMASINA?'

Tommy ignored the voice calling her. 'Go, Sir Benedict!' she whispered.

'Thomasina!'

Tommy knew it would be Mrs Moon, the cook, angry because she wasn't standing at the long table peeling mountains of potatoes with the other kitchen girls. Instead, Tommy was standing at the kitchen

doorway, watching the knights practising in the great courtyard.

Clank, clank. The courtyard rang with the sound of sword against armour.

Sir Benedict and another knight, Sir Hugh, were teaching the squires how to fight.

'Now I thrust,' Sir Benedict called. He lunged forward with his sword.

Sir Hugh then drove his sword at Sir Benedict.

'Now I parry,' Sir Benedict explained, as he blocked the blow with his own sword.

The squires, who were boys training to be knights, copied Sir Benedict's moves with their wooden practice swords. So did Tommy, with the small paring knife she was meant to be using on the potatoes.

'Hooray!' Tommy cheered softly as Sir Benedict, Flamant Castle's bravest knight, raised his sword to signal the end of practice. The sun glinted off the steel blade, and for a moment Tommy imagined that she was the one holding her sword aloft. That she was the castle's most daring knight, its most skilled sword fighter.

'Ouch!' Tommy cried, as a hand grasped her ear and twisted it hard.

'So there you are, Thomasina,' Mrs Moon scolded. 'I should have known you'd be watching the knights again. You're meant to be peeling potatoes, not dreaming in doorways.'

'Sorry, Mrs Moon,' Tommy murmured. She turned to follow the cook back into the gloomy kitchen with its smoke-blackened stone walls.

But Mrs Moon blocked her way. 'Not so fast, girl. I've got another job for you. Since you clearly prefer the courtyard to the kitchen, you can sweep it.' She thrust a broom at Tommy.

Tommy gaped at the cook in astonishment. 'Sweep the whole courtyard? But the courtyard is huge! It will take me forever!'

'You'd best get started then,' Mrs Moon said.

With a sigh, Tommy took the broom. As the knights led the squires away, she trudged across the flagstones to the far side of the courtyard. The castle walls and towers reared high above her, and she could just see the guards keeping lookout from the battlements.

'I bet those guards don't care whether the courtyard is dusty,' Tommy grumbled to herself as she began to sweep. 'And I bet the knights don't either. They're worried about more important things, like keeping Sir Walter's castle and lands safe.' Flamant Castle belonged to Sir Walter the Bald and his wife, Lady Beatrix the Bored.

Tommy was so busy grumbling that she didn't notice what was going on nearby until she heard an indignant yowl.

Looking up, she saw a stocky boy with bright red hair. Tommy had seen him before, though she had never spoken to him. He was one of the boys who worked in the armoury, where all the weapons and armour were repaired and stored.

'Don't know what he's got to yowl about,'

Tommy muttered. 'He gets to spend all day with the swords and bows while I'm scrubbing pots in the scullery and chopping vegetables in the kitchen.'

Her thoughts were interrupted by another yowl, and then a low hiss.

Tommy pushed her mop of hair out of her eyes and looked at the boy again. This time she noticed that he was holding one of the wooden practice swords. He was jabbing the tip of the sword at a black and white cat he'd trapped in a corner, and it was the cat who was yowling.

'Hey!' Tommy called. 'You leave that cat alone.'

The red-haired boy turned around. 'Who's going to make me?' he sneered. 'You?' He jabbed the cat again.

This time the cat mewed

pitifully and Tommy, who loved animals, ran towards the pair.

'Stop!' she cried. 'You're hurting it.'

The boy spun around and pointed the sword at Tommy. 'Who are you?' he demanded.

'I'm – I'm Tommy. I work in the kitchen.'

'A kitchen girl?' said the boy. He laughed rudely. 'Well I don't take orders from kitchen girls – I'm Keeper of the Bows. I'm in charge of all the castle's crossbows and longbows. What are you in charge of?' His gaze fell on the broom

Tommy was still holding in one hand. 'Ha! I know – you're Keeper of the Brooms!' He snorted with laughter at his own joke, then said, 'Go away, kitchen girl, I'm practising my sword fighting.'

He turned and lunged towards the cat. Tommy sprang forward and with her free hand grabbed the hem of his tunic.

With an angry shout the boy pushed Tommy away roughly. 'Would you rather I practise on you?' he said.

'At least it would be a fair fight,' Tommy snapped.

'A fair fight?' scoffed the boy. 'How dare you presume to be my equal! Get lost, kitchen girl.' And then he lifted his sword above his head and spun on his heel.

As the wooden blade tore through the air towards the cat cowering against the stones, Tommy leaped forward. Flinging herself between the boy and the cat, she halted the sword's arc with the broomstick.

'I warned you!' he snarled, before swinging his arm back and driving his blade straight at Tommy.

97

ABOUT THE AUTHOR

FRANCES WATTS was born in the medieval city of Lausanne, in Switzerland, and moved to Australia when she was three. After studying literature at university she began working as an editor. Her bestselling picture books include *Kisses for Daddy* and the 2008 Children's Book Council of Australia award-winner, *Parsley Rabbit's Book about Books* (both illustrated by David Legge). Frances is also the author of a series about two very unlikely superheroes, Extraordinary Ernie and Marvellous Maud, and the highly acclaimed children's fantasy/adventure series, the Gerander Trilogy.

Frances lives in Sydney's inner west, and divides her time between writing and editing. Her cat doesn't talk.

ABOUT THE ILLUSTRATOR

GREGORY ROGERS has always loved art and drawing so it's no surprise he became an illustrator. He was the first Australian to win the prestigious Kate Greenaway Medal. The first of his popular wordless picture book series, *The Boy, the Bear, the Baron, the Bard*, was selected as one of the Ten Best Illustrated Picture Books of 2004 by the *New York Times* and short-listed for the Children's Book Council of Australia Book of the Year Award in 2005. The third book, *The Hero of Little Street*, won the CBCA Picture Book of the Year in 2010. Gregory loves movies and music, and is a collector of books, antiques and anything odd and unusual.

He lives in Brisbane above a bookshop cafe with his cat Sybil.

Tournament
TROUBLE

'I want you to fight in the tournament, Tommy.'

Flamant Castle is having a tournament! But when one
of the squires is injured during practice, Sir Benedict
asks Tommy to take his place. He even offers her one
of his own horses to ride. It's a dream come true for
Tommy. There's just one problem: she has never ridden
a horse before – and every time she tries to ride Bess,
the horse throws her off! Time is running out …
How will Tommy be able to compete?

COMING IN SEPTEMBER 2012

THE *Siege* SCARE

'We're under siege!'

When Sir Walter, Sir Benedict and the other knights go to nearby Roses Castle for a tournament, the enemy knights from Malice attack Flamant. The only hope of rescue lies in getting a message to Sir Benedict, a day's ride away. But the castle is surrounded and there's no way out! With the help of her friends, Tommy devises a daring plan. Can she save Flamant Castle before it's too late?

COMING IN SEPTEMBER 2012